The Crazy Critters' Cooking Convention

Written by Greg Banks

Illustrated by Kelvin Hawley

Anton Ant arrived on an antelope.

Betty Butterfly bounced up on a bear.

2

Dennis Dragonfly drifted in on his donkey.

Florence Firefly flew in on a fish.

3

Gregory Grasshopper grabbed on to his gorilla.

Molly Mosquito marched in on her manatee.

4

Patrick Praying Mantis pranced in on a panda.

Sarah Spider slipped off a shaggy sheep.

Tommy Termite traveled on a turtle.

Wanda Wasp wandered in on a walrus.

Candice Cow called out,
"Let the Crazy Critters' Cooking
Convention commence!"

So Florence fried
and Sarah stirred.

Molly mixed and Gregory grated.
Wanda whisked and Betty baked.

Then Candice Cow called out,
"Let the eating begin!"

So Anton ate apple pie.

Betty bit on bacon burgers.

Dennis devoured dates.

Florence fed on French fries.

Gregory gobbled garlic.

Molly munched mulberry muffins.

Patrick picked at pizza.
Sarah sipped soda.

Tommy tasted tuna tortillas.
Wanda wolfed down waffles.

16

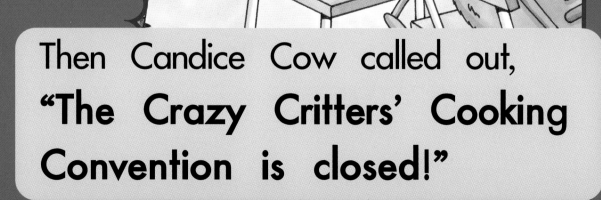

Then Candice Cow called out, "The Crazy Critters' Cooking Convention is closed!"

So Anton got on his antelope.

And Betty got on her bear.

Dennis got on his donkey, and Florence got on her fish.

Gregory grabbed his gorilla,
and Molly got on her manatee.

Patrick got on his panda,
and Sarah got on her sheep.

Tommy got on his turtle,
and Wanda got on her walrus.

"Bring a friend with you next year," called Candice Cow.

Who will go to the next
Crazy Critters' Cooking Convention?